East o' the Sun & West o' the Moon

AN OLD NORSE TALE

TRANSLATED BY

SIR GEORGE WEBBE DASENT

ILLUSTRATED BY

GILLIAN BARLOW

PHILOMEL BOOKS

NEW YORK

For Michael and Eleni

7891757 Nosh

Copyright © 1988 by Gillian Barlow.
Published by Philomel Books,
a division of The Putnam & Grosset Group,
200 Madison Avenue, New York, NY 10016.
All rights reserved.
Published simultaneously in Canada.
Printed in Hong Kong by South China Printing Co.
Book design by Nanette Stevenson.

Library of Congress Cataloging-in-Publication Data
East o' the sun and west o' the moon / illustrated by Gillian Barlow.
p.   cm.   Summary: A girl travels east of the sun and west of
the moon to free her beloved prince from a magic spell.
ISBN 0-399-21570-0
[1. Fairy tales. 2. Folklore—Norway.] I. Barlow, Gillian, ill.
PZ8.E119 1988   398.2—dc19   [E]   87-32679   CIP   AC

First impression

ONCE UPON A TIME there was a poor husbandman who had so many children that he hadn't much of either food or clothing to give them. Pretty children they all were, but the prettiest was the youngest daughter, who was so lovely there was no end to her loveliness.

So one day—'twas on a Thursday evening late at the fall of the year—the weather was so wild and rough outside, and it was so cruelly dark, and rain fell and wind blew, till the walls of the cottage shook again—there they all sat around the fire busy with this thing and that. But just then, all at once something gave three taps on the windowpane.

Then the father went out to see what was the matter; and, when he got out of doors, what should he see but a great big White Bear.

"Good evening to you!" said the White Bear.

"The same to you," said the man.

"Will you give me your youngest daughter? If you will, I'll make you as rich as you now are poor," said the Bear.

Well, the man would not be at all sorry to be as rich as that, but still he thought he must have a bit of a talk with his daughter first; so he went in and told her how there was a great White Bear waiting outside, who had given his word to make them so rich if he could only have the youngest daughter.

The lassie said "No!" outright. Nothing could get her to say anything else; so the man went out and settled it with the White Bear, that he should come again the next Thursday evening and get an answer. Meantime he talked his daughter over, and kept on telling her of all the riches they would get, and how well off she would be herself; and so at last she thought better of it, and washed and mended her rags, made herself as smart as she could, and was ready to start. I can't say her packing gave her much trouble.

Next Thursday evening came the White Bear to fetch her, and she got up on his back with her bundle, and off they went. So, when they had gone a bit of the way, the White Bear said:

"Are you afraid?"

No! she wasn't.

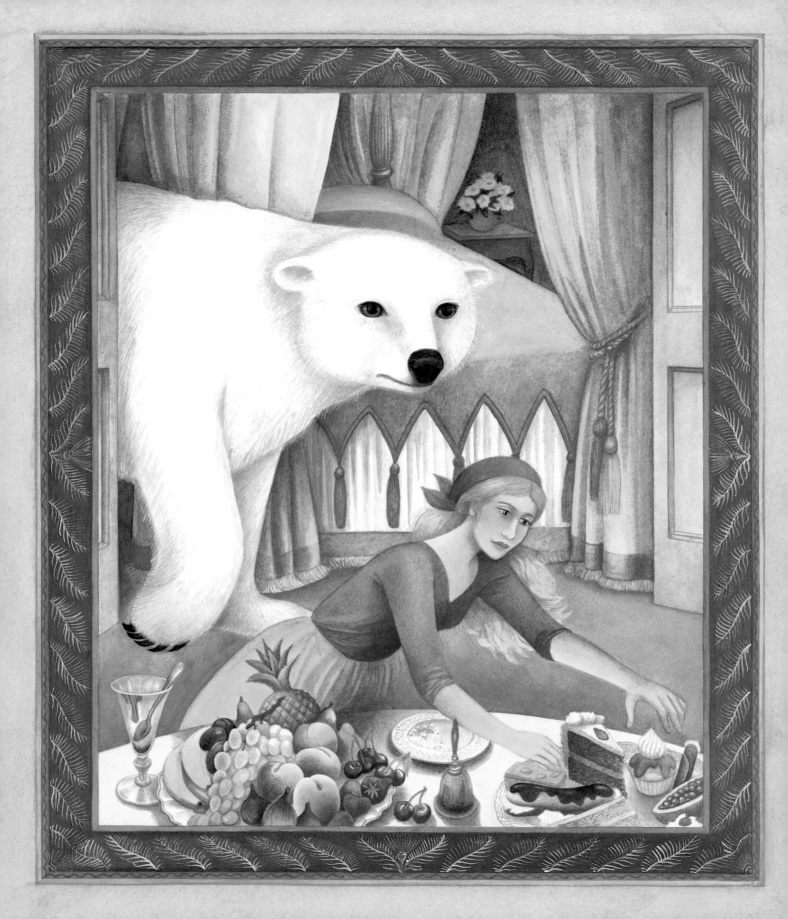

"Well! Mind and hold tight by my shaggy coat, and then there's nothing to fear," said the Bear.

So she rode a long, long way, till they came to a great steep hill. There, on the face of it, the White Bear gave a knock, and a door opened, and they came into a castle, where there were many rooms all lit up, rooms gleaming with silver and gold; and there too was a table ready laid, and it was all as grand as grand could be. Then the White Bear gave her a silver bell; and when she wanted anything, she was only to ring it, and she would get it at once.

Well, after she had eaten and drunk, and evening wore on, she got sleepy after her journey, and thought she would like to go to bed, so she rang the bell; and she had scarce taken hold of it before she came into a chamber, where there was a bed made, as fair and white as any one would wish to sleep in, with silken pillows and curtains, and gold fringe. All that was in the room was gold or silver; but when she had gone to bed, and put out the light, a man came and laid himself alongside of her. That was the White Bear, who threw off his beast shape at night; but she never saw him for he always came after she had put out the light, and before the day dawned he was up and off again.

So things went on happily for a while, but at last she began to get silent and sorrowful, for there she went about all day alone, and she longed to go home to see her father and mother, and brothers and sisters. So one day, when the White Bear asked what it was that she lacked, she said it was so dull and lonely there, and how she longed to go home to see her father and mother, and brothers and sisters, and

that was why she was so sad and sorrowful, because she couldn't get to them.

"Well, well!" said the Bear. "Perhaps there's a cure for all this; but you must promise me one thing, not to talk alone with your mother, but only when the rest are by to hear, for she'll take you by the hand and try to lead you into a room alone to talk; but you must mind and not do that, else you'll bring bad luck on both of us."

So one Sunday the White Bear came and said now they could set off to see her father and mother. Well, off they started, she sitting on his back; and they went far and long. At last they came to a grand house, and there her brothers and sisters were running about out of doors at play, and everything was so pretty, 'twas a joy to see.

"This is where your father and mother live now," said the White Bear; "but don't forget what I told you, else you'll make us both unlucky."

No! bless her, she'd not forget; and when she had reached the house, the White Bear turned right about and left her.

Then when she went in to see her father and mother, there was such joy, there was no end to it. None of them thought they could thank her enough for all she had done for them. Now, they had everything they wished, as good as good could be, and they all wanted to know how she got on where she lived.

Well, she said, it was very good to live where she did; she had all she wished. What she said beside I don't know; but I don't think any of them had the right end of the stick, or that they got much out of

her. But so in the afternoon, after they had done dinner, all happened as the White Bear had said. Her mother wanted to talk with her alone in her bedroom; but she minded what the White Bear had said, and wouldn't go upstairs.

"Oh! What we have to talk about, will keep," she said, and put her mother off. But somehow or other, her mother got round her at last, and she had to tell her the whole story. So she said, how every night, when she had gone to bed, a man came and lay down beside her as soon as she had put out the light, and how she never saw him, because he was always up and away before the morning dawned; and how she went about woeful and sorrowing, for she thought she should so like to see him, and how all day long she walked about there alone, and how dull, and dreary, and lonesome it was.

"My!" said her mother; "It may well be a Troll you slept with! But now I'll teach you a lesson how to set eyes on him. I'll give you a bit of candle, which you can carry home in your bosom; just light that while he is asleep, but take care not to drop the tallow on him."

Yes! She took the candle, and hid it in her bosom, and as night drew on, the White Bear came and fetched her away.

But when they had gone a bit of the way, the White Bear asked if all hadn't happened as he had said?

Well, she couldn't say it hadn't.

"Now, mind," said he, "if you have listened to your mother's advice, you have brought bad luck on us both, and then, all that has passed between us will be as nothing."

No, she said, she hadn't listened to her mother's advice.

So when she reached home, and had gone to bed, it was the old story over again. There came a man and lay down beside her; but at dead of night, when she heard he slept, she got up and struck a light, lit the candle, and let the light shine on him, and so she saw that he was the loveliest prince one ever set eyes on, and she fell so deep in love with him on the spot, that she thought she couldn't live if she didn't give him a kiss there and then. And so she did, but as she kissed him, she dropped three hot drops of tallow on his shirt, and he woke up.

"What have you done?" he cried. "Now you have made us both unlucky, for had you held out only this one year, I had been freed. For I have a stepmother who has bewitched me, so that I am a White Bear by day, and a Man by night. But now all ties are snapped between us; now I must set off from you to her. She lives in a castle which stands East o' the Sun and West o' the Moon, and there, too, is a Princess, with a nose three ells long, and she's the wife I must have now."

She wept and took it ill, but there was no help for it; go he must.

Then she asked if she mightn't go with him?

No, she mightn't.

"Tell me the way, then," she said, "and I'll search you out; *that* surely I may get leave to do."

Yes, she might do that, he said; but there was no way to that place. It lay East o' the Sun and West o' the Moon, and thither she'd never find her way.

So next morning, when she woke up, both Prince and castle were gone, and there she lay on a little green patch, in the midst of the gloomy thick wood, and by her side lay the same bundle of rags she had brought with her from her old home.

So when she had rubbed the sleep out of her eyes, and wept till she was tired, she set out on her way, and walked many, many days, till she came to a lofty crag. Under it sat an old hag, and played with a gold apple which she tossed about. The lassie asked her if she knew the way to the Prince, who lived with his stepmother in the castle, that lay East o' the Sun and West o' the Moon, and who was to marry the Princess with a nose three ells long.

"How did you come to know about him?" asked the old hag; "but maybe you are the lassie who ought to have had him?"

Yes, she was.

"So, so; it's you, is it?" said the old hag. "Well, all I know about him is, that he lives in the castle that lies East o' the Sun and West o' the Moon, and thither you'll come, late or never; but still you may have the loan of my horse, and on him you can ride to my next neighbour. Maybe she'll be able to tell you; and when you get there, just give the horse a switch under the left ear, and beg him to be off home. And, stay, this gold apple you may take with you."

So she got up on the horse, and rode a long, long time, till she came to another crag, under which sat another old hag, with a gold carding comb. The lassie asked her if she knew the way to the castle that lay East o' the Sun and West o' the Moon, and she answered, like

the first old hag, that she knew nothing about it, except it was East o' the Sun and West o' the Moon.

"And thither you'll come, late or never, but you shall have the loan of my horse to my next neighbour. Maybe she'll tell you all about it; and when you get there, just switch the horse under the left ear, and beg him to be off home."

And this old hag gave her the golden carding comb; it might be she'd find some use for it, she said. So the lassie got up on the horse, and rode a far, far way, and a weary time; and so at last she came to another great crag, under which sat another old hag, spinning with a golden spinning wheel. Here, too, she asked if she knew the way to the Prince, and where the castle was that lay East o' the Sun and West o' the Moon. So it was the same thing over again.

"Maybe it's you who ought to have had the Prince?" said the old hag.

Yes, it was.

But she, too, didn't know the way a bit better than the other two. "East o' the Sun and West o' the Moon it was," she knew—that was all.

"And thither you'll come, late or never; but I'll lend you my horse, and then I think you'd best ride to the East Wind and ask him. Maybe he knows those parts, and can blow you thither. But when you get to him, you need only give the horse a switch under the left ear, and he'll trot home himself."

And so, too, she gave her the gold spinning wheel. "Maybe you'll find a use for it," said the old hag.

Then on she rode many, many days, a weary time, before she got to the East Wind's house, but at last she did reach it, and then she asked the East Wind if he could tell her the way to the Prince who dwelt East o' the Sun and West o' the Moon. Yes, the East Wind had often heard tell of it, the Prince and the castle, but he couldn't tell the way, for he had never blown so far.

"But, if you will, I'll go with you to my brother the West Wind, maybe he knows, for he's much stronger. So, if you will just get on my back, I'll carry you thither."

Yes, she got on his back, and I should just think they went briskly along.

So when they got there, they went into the West Wind's house, and the East Wind said the lassie he had brought was the one who ought to have had the Prince who lived in the castle East o' the Sun and West o' the Moon; and so she had set out to seek him, and how he had come with her, and would be glad to know if the West Wind knew how to get to the castle.

"Nay," said the West Wind, "so far I've never blown; but if you will, I'll go with you to our brother the South Wind, for he's much stronger than either of us, and he has flapped his wings far and wide. Maybe he'll tell you. You can get on my back, and I'll carry you to him."

Yes! she got on his back, and so they travelled to the South Wind, and weren't very long on the way, either.

When they got there, the West Wind asked him if he could tell her

the way to the castle that lay East o' the Sun and West o' the Moon, for it was she who ought to have had the Prince who lived there.

"You don't say so! That's the one, is it?" said the South Wind.

"Well, I've blustered about in most places in my time, but so far I've never blown; but if you will, I'll take you to my brother the North Wind. He is the oldest and strongest of the whole lot of us, and if he don't know where it is, you'll never find any one in the world to tell you. You can get on my back, and I'll carry you thither."

Yes! she got on his back, and away he went from his house at a fine rate. And this time, too, she wasn't long on her way.

So when they got near the North Wind's house, he was so wild and cross, that they could feel cold puffs of air coming at them on the way.

"BLAST YOU BOTH, WHAT DO YOU WANT?" he roared out to them ever so far off, so that it struck them with an icy shiver.

"Well," said the South Wind, "you needn't be so foul-mouthed, for here I am, your brother, the South Wind, and here is the lassie who ought to have had the Prince who dwells in the castle that lies East o' the Sun and West o' the Moon, and now she wants to ask you if you ever were there, and can tell her the way, for she would be so glad to find him again."

"Yes, I know well enough where it is," said the North Wind. "Once in my life I blew an aspen leaf thither, but I was so tired I couldn't blow a puff for ever so many days after. But if you really wish to go there, and aren't afraid to come along with me, I'll take you on my back and see if I can blow you thither."

Yes! with all her heart; she must and would get there if it were possible in any way, and as for fear, however madly he went, she wouldn't be at all afraid.

"Very well, then," said the North Wind, "but you must sleep here tonight, for we must have the whole day before us, if we're to get thither at all."

Early next morning the North Wind woke her, and puffed himself up, and blew himself out, and made himself so stout and big, 'twas gruesome to look at him; and so off they went high up through the air, as if they would never stop till they got to the world's end.

Down here below there was such a storm; it threw down long tracts of wood and many houses, and when it swept over the great sea, ships foundered by hundreds.

So they tore on and on—no one can believe how far they went— and all the while they still went over the sea, and the North Wind got more and more weary, and so out of breath he could scarce bring out a puff, and his wings dropped and dropped, till at last he sunk so low that the crests of the waves dashed over his heels.

"Are you afraid?" said the North Wind.

No! she wasn't.

But they weren't very far from land; and the North Wind had still so much strength left in him that he managed to throw her up on the shore under the windows of the castle which lay East o' the Sun and West o' the Moon, but then he was so weak and worn out, he had to stay there and rest many days before he could get home again.

Next morning the lassie sat down under the castle window, and began to play with the gold apple; and the first person she saw was the Longnose who was to have the Prince.

"What do you want for your gold apple, you lassie?" said the Longnose, and threw up the window.

"It's not for sale, for gold or money," said the lassie.

"If it's not for sale for gold or money, what is it that you will sell it for? You may name your own price," said the Princess.

"Well! if I may get to the Prince, who lives here, and be with him tonight, you shall have it," said the lassie whom the North Wind had brought.

Yes! she might; that could be done. So the Princess got the apple; but when the lassie came up to the Prince's bedroom at night he was fast asleep. She called him and shook him, and between whiles she wept sore; but for all she could do she couldn't wake him up. Next morning as soon as day broke, came the Princess with the long nose, and drove her out again.

So in the daytime she sat down under the castle window and began to card with her golden carding comb, and the same thing happened. The Princess asked what she wanted for it; and she said it wasn't for sale for gold or money, but if she might get leave to go up to the Prince and be with him that night, the Princess should have it. But when she went up she found him fast asleep again, and for all she called, and all she shook, and wept, and prayed, she couldn't get life into him; and as soon as the first gray peep of day came, then came the

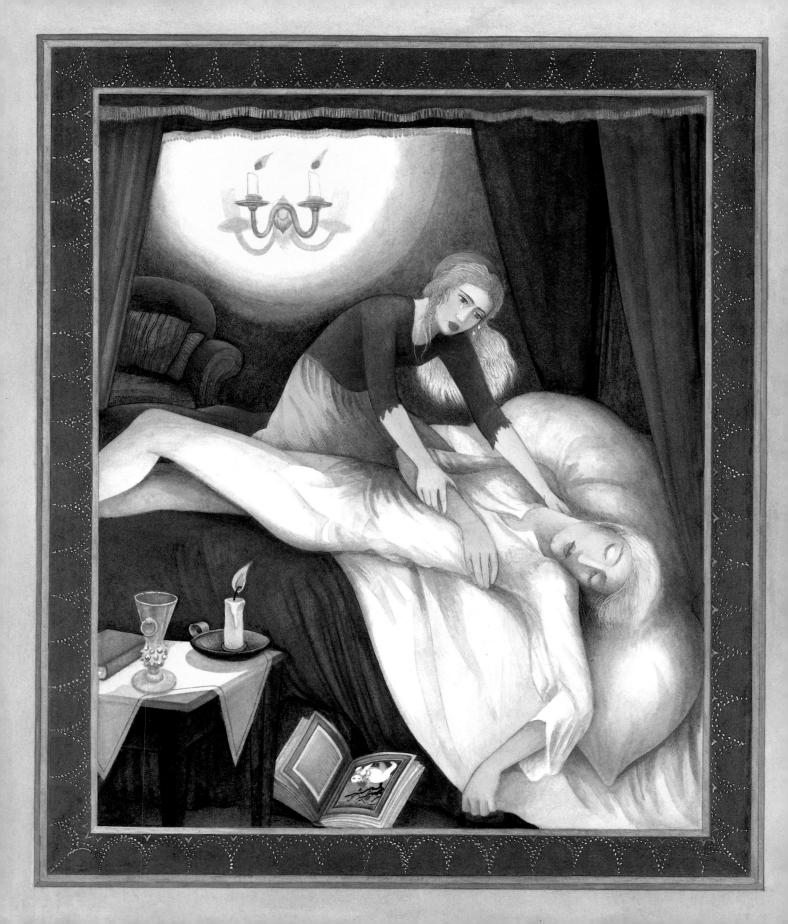

Princess with the long nose, and chased her out again.

So, in the daytime, the lassie sat down outside under the castle window, and began to spin with her golden spinning wheel, and that, too, the Princess with the long nose wanted to have. So she threw up the window and asked what she wanted for it. The lassie said, as she had said twice before, it wasn't for sale for gold or money; but if she might go up to the Prince who was there, and be with him alone that night, she might have it.

Yes! she might do that and welcome. But now you must know there were some other good folk who had been carried off thither, and as they sat in their room, which was next the Prince, they had heard how a woman had been in there, and wept and prayed, and called to him two nights running, and they told that to the Prince.

That evening, when the Princess came with her sleepy drink, the Prince made as if he drank, but threw it over his shoulder, for he could guess it was a sleepy drink. So, when the lassie came in, she found the Prince wide awake; and then she told him the whole story how she had come thither.

"Ah," said the Prince, "you've just come in the very nick of time, for tomorrow is to be my wedding day; but now I won't have the Longnose, and you are the only woman in the world who can set me free. I'll say I want to see what my wife is fit for, and beg her to wash the shirt which has the three spots of tallow on it; she'll say yes, for she doesn't know 'tis you who put them there. But that's a work only for good human folk, and not for such a pack of Trolls, and so I'll say that

I won't have any other for my bride than the woman who can wash them out, and ask you to do it."

So there was great joy and love between them all that night. But next day, when the wedding was to be, the Prince said:

"First of all, I'd like to see what my bride is fit for."

"Yes!" said the stepmother, with all her heart.

"Well," said the Prince, "I've got a fine shirt which I'd like for my wedding shirt, but somehow or other it has got three spots of tallow on it, which I must have washed out; and I have sworn never to take any other bride than the woman who's able to do that. If she can't, she's not worth having."

Well, that was no great thing they said, so they agreed, and she with the long nose began to wash away as hard as she could, but the more she rubbed and scrubbed, the bigger the spots grew.

"Ah!" said the old hag, her mother, "You can't wash; let me try."

But she hadn't long taken the shirt in hand, before it got far worse than ever, and with all her rubbing, and wringing, and scrubbing, the spots grew bigger and blacker, and the darker and uglier was the shirt.

Then all the other Trolls began to wash, but the longer it lasted, the blacker and uglier the shirt grew, till at last it was black all over as if it had been up the chimney.

"Ah!" said the Prince, "You're none of you worth a straw: you can't wash. Why there, outside sits a beggar lassie. I'll be bound she knows how to wash better than the whole lot of you. COME IN, LASSIE!" he shouted.

Well, in she came.

"Can you wash this shirt clean, lassie, you?" said he.

"I don't know," she said, "but I think I can."

And almost before she had taken it and dipped it in the water, it was as white as driven show, and whiter still.

"Yes, you are the lassie for me," said the Prince.

At that the old hag flew into such a rage, she burst on the spot, and the Princess with the long nose after her, and the whole pack of Trolls after her—at least I've never heard a word about them since.

As for the Prince and Princess, they set free all the poor good folk who had been carried off and shut up there; and they took with them all the silver and gold, and flitted away as far as they could from the castle that lay East o' the Sun and West o' the Moon.

THE END

A Word About the Text

"THE TASTE OF THE WORLD which has veered so often is constant enough to fairy tale. . . . They are true to the human being's early loves, they have his unblunted edge of belief and his fresh appetite for marvels." So wrote Andrew Lang in the introduction to *The Blue Fairy Book* in 1889. In this first "colour book" Lang, scholar and an active member of the Folklore Society, compiled significant tales from around the world, including Scotland, Norway, and Germany. In the original book the Norse tale *East o' the Sun and West o' the Moon* was placed third. It was switched to first in a reissue of the tales in 1975. The translation used in this volume is believed to have retained even more of the original rhythm and tone of oral language than the version used in the first *Blue Fairy Book;* translated by Sir George Webbe Dasent, this version was first published in English in 1859, appearing in *Popular Tales from the Norse.*